Written by Jennifer Gaither
Illustrated by Romont Willy

Copyright © 2023 by Puppy Dogs & Ice Cream, Inc.
All rights reserved. Published in the United States
by Puppy Dogs & Ice Cream, Inc.

ISBN: 978-1-957922-57-7
Edition: January 2023

PDIC and Puppy Dogs & Ice Cream are trademarks
of Puppy Dogs & Ice Cream, Inc.

For all inquiries, please contact us at:
info@puppysmiles.org

To see more of our books, visit us at:
www.PuppyDogsAndIceCream.com

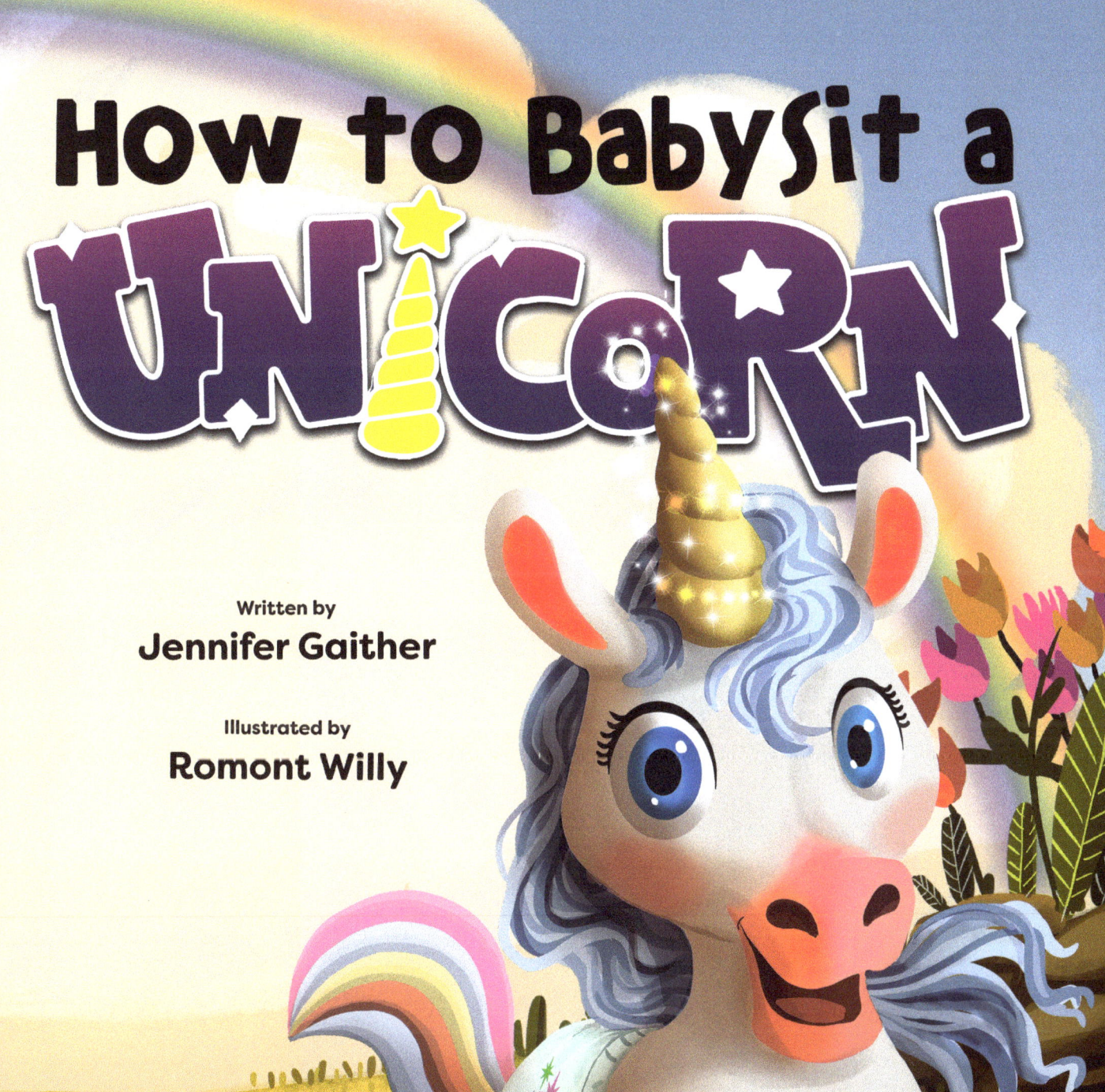

The office phone rings, a call's coming through.
"We are The Babysitters, the magic HQ!"
A WHIMSICAL whisper floats over the air,
"We need a great sitter for unicorn care!"

"My husband and I have a mission at hand;
Our **POWERS** are needed to rescue the land.
Do you have a sitter who can handle our foal?
She needs to be nice, but maintain control."

"Let me look through our pages, please hold on a sec...
She's an excellent fit, yes, we'll send over Bec.
Becca really loves HORSES, she's stern, but still kind.
She's magic with ponies, like you have in mind."

Becca crosses the rainbow, floats down on a cloud,
Into a green forest, where few are allowed.
Set there, in the mountain, a stone cottage hides,
The place where a unicorn family resides.

The door rockets open with SPARKLES and light,
And Becca's reaction is of pure delight.
Their long, silky manes seem to flow in the breeze,
And their hooves cross the ground with ethereal ease.

"We'll be gone for the **day**,
and return in the **night**.
We have three simple rules
to make sure this goes right:
No jumping indoors,
stay inside when it's dark,
And no making messes
with our little Spark."
Mr. and Mrs.
take off to the sky,
Leaving Becca to wonder
if foals also fly...

What games can you PLAY with a young unicorn?
Becca tosses a horseshoe around the foal's horn.
Then Spark wants to play "Pin the tail on the friend."
But Becca's unsure about how that might end!

They read a few books, they draw, and they bake,
A unicorn cupcake, what else would they make?
Then Spark's getting cranky, it's time that they eat.
Bec searches the pantry, while Spark takes a seat.

The options are endless! The pantry's all treats.
There're berries with sugar, and bright, **FIZZING** sweets.
Cookies and sodas, no veggies in sight.
For unicorn supper, would this be alright?

But Spark is so hungry, so Becca lets loose.
The **RAVENOUS** pony guzzles cupcakes and juice.
Soon after, the kitchen is in quite a state –
There are dishes and wrappers, and tall stacks of plates.

They both broke a rule! Spark lets out a big yawn.
Then she waves her horn, and the mess is all GONE!
"Where did it go?" An astonished Bec asks.
"Somewhere else!" Giggles Spark, as she nods towards the grass.

The unicorn foal ROLLS around on the ground, And Becca begs Spark, "Won't you please settle down?"

She fetches a comb and some COLORFUL bows.
Then braids the foal's mane into plaits and neat rows.

"Time to brush your teeth, Spark!" But Spark sure doesn't care.
And before Becca knows it, she jumps in the air.
Spark, still just a pony, then quickly goes reeling.
And **"THWACK!"** Her horn sticks in the glittering ceiling.

Overwhelmed, Becca sighs, "Well, there goes another rule."
With the pony's horn stuck, she cannot lose her cool.
Spark cries as her hooves *wiggle* far off the ground,
And her unicorn magic makes things zoom around.

"Don't worry, I promise, I'll get you down now!"
Becca looks for a way she can do that, somehow.
Becca sets to work braiding, then lasso's Spark's hoof,
And "**POP**" Becca yanks the foal loose from the roof.

The sun has now set, and the stars twinkle bright,
And it's time to sing Spark a sleepy "Goodnight"
Bec reads her a book, "Sleep Tight, Unicorn,"
As the foal rests her head and her little horn.

Bec rushes around, she's a **WHIRLWIND** that cleans.
So Mr. and Mrs. won't see such a scene!
The parents arrive, they're exhausted and spent,
They smile down at Becca, and ask how things went.

Sheepishly, Becca points out the new HOLE
Made from a certain young unicorn foal.
"You're patient and kind, and she's headstrong, we know,
When you're watching Spark, that's just how some things go."

Becca hops on the cloud, and sails into the night,
Her heart filled with magic, and Spark sleeping tight.
No job is too big, no sitter a quitter,
For a **magical** time – call on The Babysitters!

Claim your FREE Gift!

 Visit:

PDICBooks.com/Gift

Thank you for purchasing

and welcome to the Puppy Dogs & Ice Cream family. We're certain you're going to love the little gift we've prepared for you at the website above.

Printed in the USA
CPSIA information can be obtained
at www.ICGtesting.com
LVHW071135261023
762204LV00013B/338

Malia's Magnificent Moontime

A Holistic Guide to Menstrual Self-Care

By Angela Shabazz & Kendi Shabazz Muhammad

No part of this book or its images may be reproduced in any form or by any electronic or mechanical means including information storage and retrieval systems, without permission in writing from the authors. This book is a work of fiction. Names, characters, places, and incidents either are products of the author's imagination. Any resemblance to actual persons, living or dead, events, or locales is entirely coincidental.

Copyright © 2016 IWS Publishing

ISBN-13: 978-0692656020

ISBN-10: 0692656022

This book is dedicated to Kendi, the person who helped dictate this book to me. Thank you for this lovely gift. I suspect many young ladies will be positively impacted by it. You were, are, and will always be "the loved one," "the cream," and "the one who is praiseworthy."

Life can change in the blink of an eye, as Malia found out one lovely Tuesday afternoon. Malia and her sister, Aisha sat on their back porch laughing and playing with Aisha's stuffed toys. The warm sun beamed down, coaxing their skin into deeper shades of bronze, while the honeysuckle scented breeze relieved the mid-summer heat.

"Ouch!" Suddenly, Malia felt an ache in her belly. She bent over and held her stomach. "Owww! I'm going to go inside, Aisha. I don't feel well," said Malia.

"Okay. I hope you feel better!" the younger sister replied. Aisha enjoyed playing with her big sister and was eager for her to get well.

Malia traipsed inside, her thick honey-brown locs bouncing with every weary step.

"Where's Aisha?" Momma asked as she approached her daughter in the hallway. Malia was ten years old and Aisha had just turned five. Momma was amazed by how fast her daughters were growing up.

"She's still outside playing. I want to lie down because my stomach hurts," Malia replied.

Momma grew concerned as she moved her cobalt-colored bangles further up her cocoa arms to feel Malia's head for signs of a fever. Her head felt cool. Together, they walked upstairs to the girl's bedroom. Momma pulled up the soft, lavender blanket to tuck Malia in for a nap.

"You don't have a fever. Hopefully, you will feel well soon. Go, get some rest. Granny is coming over later and you don't want to miss the fun! I'll be back to check on you in a while," Momma reassured.

A little while later Momma came to check on Malia. She gently nudged her daughter, but she was fast asleep. Waking the girls up was never easy. In fact, she suspected both girls could sleep through an earthquake without being disturbed. She patiently kept nudging until she heard Malia groan.

"Time to get up, Malia. Granny will be here soon. Are you feeling any better?"

Malia grunted as she was forced to wake up. Her belly still hurt quite a bit. As much as she wanted to sleep, she didn't want to miss her grandmother's visit. Not to mention, sometimes Granny made the girls take bitter-tasting *herbs* when they were too sick to get out of bed.

"Yes, ma'am. I'll come downstairs," she said. As Malia rushed out of bed, she looked down and saw a red stain on her pretty sheets.

"Eww! Momma, I'm bleeding!"

Momma stared at the bed in disbelief. "Don't worry. You're okay Malia. This bleeding is perfectly normal. It's time for us to have a talk, but first, let's get you cleaned up."

Although Malia's body had been going through a lot of changes, Momma felt totally unprepared. Her daughter was so young, yet she was growing up so quickly. Momma took Malia into the bathroom. She stuck a cotton pad on a pair of clean panties.

"Go ahead and wash up. When you are finished, put these on," she said as she handed Malia the panties. "I am going to go change your sheets and check on Aisha. When you are finished, come downstairs and I'll explain what's going on in your body right now. We should've had this talk earlier, but I never imagined this would happen so soon! I was thirteen when my moontime arrived."

"Moontime?" Malia said to herself as her mother left. She was quite puzzled. Malia hurried to freshen up.

Afterward, Malia went to speak with her mother. She wondered what this weird moontime thing was that her mother referred to. She had heard Momma and Granny discussing it before, yet Malia was usually too busy playing to pay attention to what they said. One thing was certain - Malia didn't like it; not one bit!

Malia found Momma seated on the front porch watching Aisha as she played with her soccer ball. She plopped down as Momma motioned for her to sit next to her.

How are you feeling?" Momma asked.

"Okay, I guess. My stomach still hurts."

"Yes, that can happen when your moontime comes. Don't worry, there are things we can do to ease the pain. Your moontime doesn't have to be uncomfortable.

Some people refer to a woman's moontime as a *period* or *menstruation*. Indigenous people call it our moontime because a woman's body cycle resembles the cycle of the moon's orbit. It takes the moon twenty-eight days to move around the Earth, which is about the time of a normal moon (*menstrual*) cycle in women. Some women have slightly shorter or longer cycles and that's okay too. For a few days in each cycle, blood flows out of a special place in your body called the *vagina*. Your *vagina* is like a secret tunnel from inside your body to the outside world. It is positioned in the space between where you urinate (pee) and defecate (poop)."

Malia thought that was strange. She never noticed any openings between her legs except the ones for using the restroom.

Momma continued, "Long ago, people were more closely in tune with nature. Women would begin their moontime when the moon was in its darkest stage, called the new moon. We would *ovulate* when the moon was in its brightest phase, called the full moon."

"What's *ovulate* mean?" asked Malia curiously.

Momma laughed, "Okay, wait. Let me back up a little bit."

Aisha grew curious about what Momma and Malia were talking about. She hated feeling left out. She crept over to the porch, hoping Momma wouldn't see her and say that she was too young to listen. She hid behind a bush where she could hear her mother speak.

"Aisha, stop sneaking around and have a seat," Momma said.

Sometimes Aisha wondered if Momma had invisible eyes in the back of her head. She always seemed to catch the girls when they were mischievous. The thought of Momma's invisible eyes made Aisha giggle. She marched out of her hiding place and sat on the steps.

"Do you know what a *womb* is?" asked Momma.

"Not really," Malia admitted.

"Nope!" Aisha added.

"Your *womb* is right here, in the lower part of your belly. It is also called your *uterus*. Your *womb* is where your babies will grow once you get married."

The thought of having a baby growing inside her was a bit strange to Malia.

"Every month a woman's body hopes to become pregnant with a baby, so it prepares itself. Your *womb* gets thick with a lining of nutrients and other good stuff to feed the baby."

"That's so weird," Aisha chuckled.

"Once the *womb* is prepared, one of your *ovaries* releases an *egg*. *Eggs* may also be called *ovum*. That *egg* starts a long voyage down the *fallopian tubes* towards the *womb*. This is called *ovulation*."

The girls tried to imagine these *eggs* inside them, and what it would be like to trek down a *fallopian tube* every month.

"Maybe," Aisha said, "It's like riding down a giant slide!"

"Maybe it's like roller skating down a long street!" Malia added.

"Perhaps the journey is like riding on a big, tall rollercoaster!" Momma chimed in with a smile. "Either way, it's a big adventure that happens in women's bodies every single month."

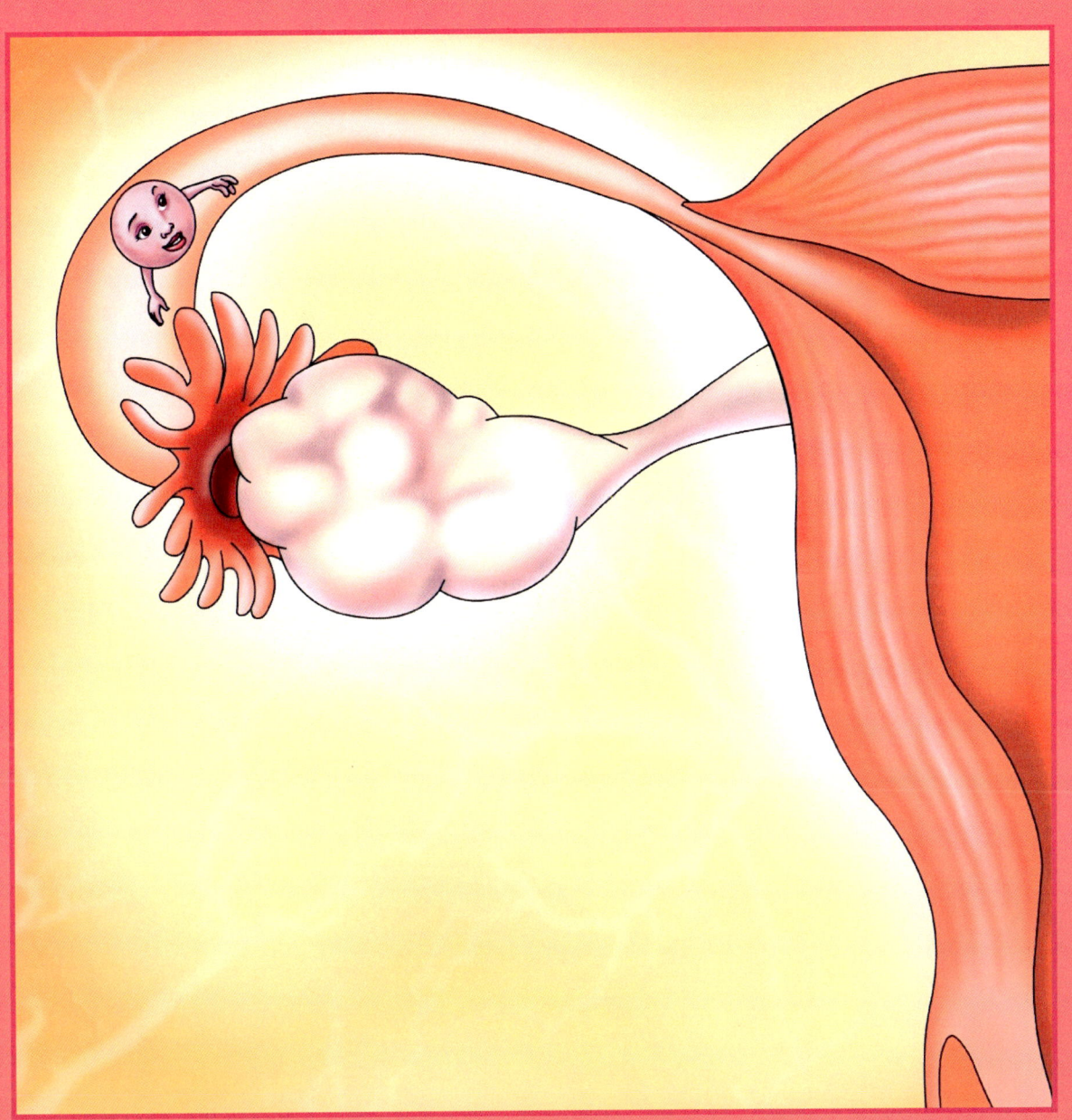

"Sometimes, a husband may place his *seed* into his wife to get her pregnant," Momma continued.

Aisha was confused. "So women have *egg*s growing inside them and men have *seed*s? This is really, really weird! Is it like an apple *seed*?" she asked, puzzled.

Momma and Aisha looked at each other and burst out laughing. "No, silly girl! A man's *seed* is made up of lots of itty-bitty cells called *sperm*. They look like tiny little tadpoles. The *sperm* swims all around the *womb* searching for the *egg*. If the *sperm* travels far enough, they reach the *fallopian tubes*. If one of the *sperm* finds the *egg*, the sperm and egg join together to create a beautiful baby. This is called *fertilization.*"

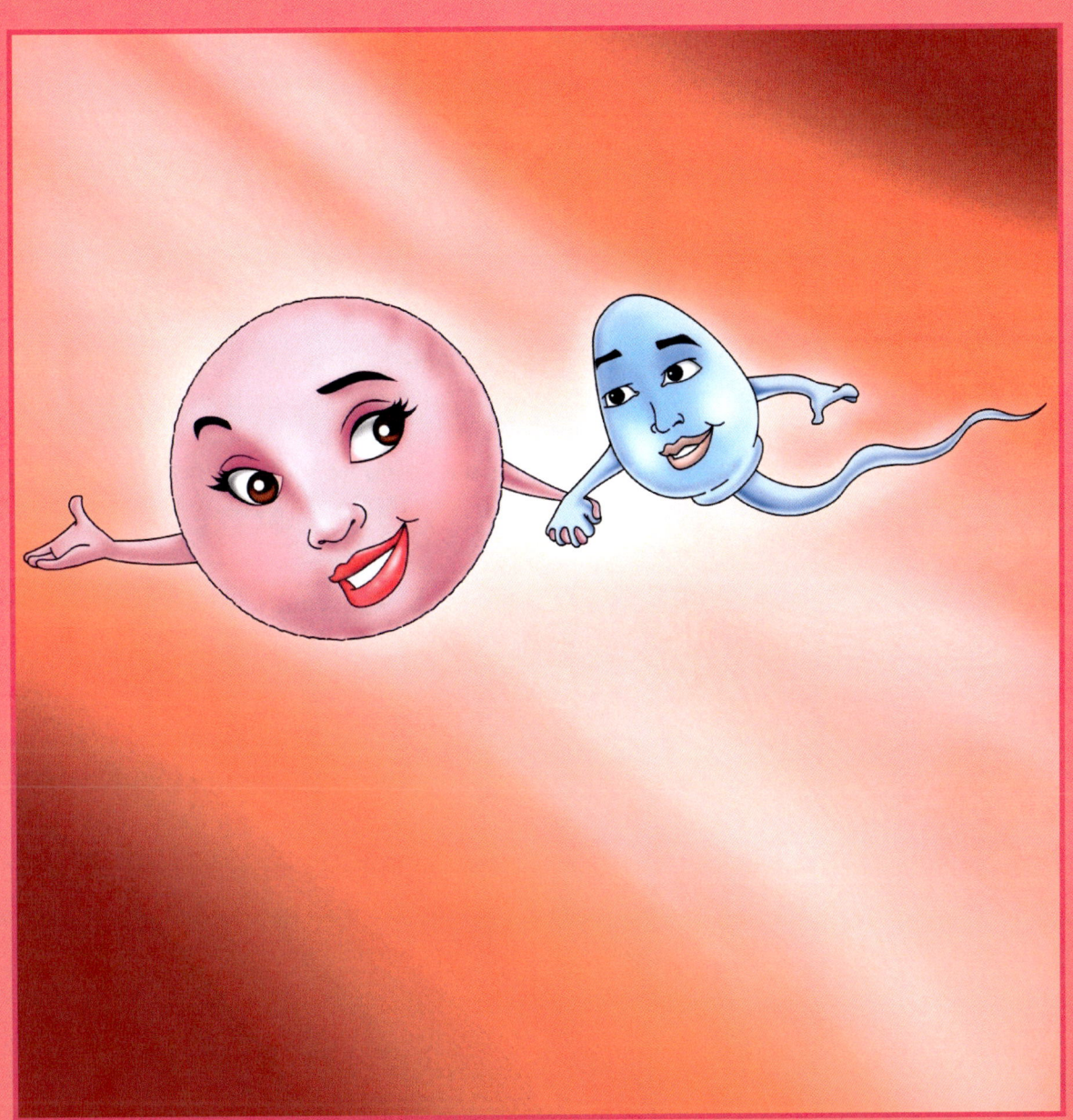

"But many times a woman doesn't have a husband to give her his *seed* or the *seed* can't find the *egg*. In this case, the *egg* never gets to become a baby, and so the *womb* sheds its lush lining, taking the *egg* with it. The extra blood and tissue flow out of the *vagina*, leaving the *womb* fresh and renewed. Once the old lining is gone, the body prepares a brand new one in hopes that it may create life during the next month.

This time of bleeding is called your moontime. Malia, your body is now able to make children. Since there is no *sperm*, your *womb* will shed its lining every month until you are blessed to get pregnant with your husband.

This cycle happens over and over again for many years. Then one day, when a woman becomes too old to carry a child, the cycle stops and she no longer bleeds. This is called *menopause*."

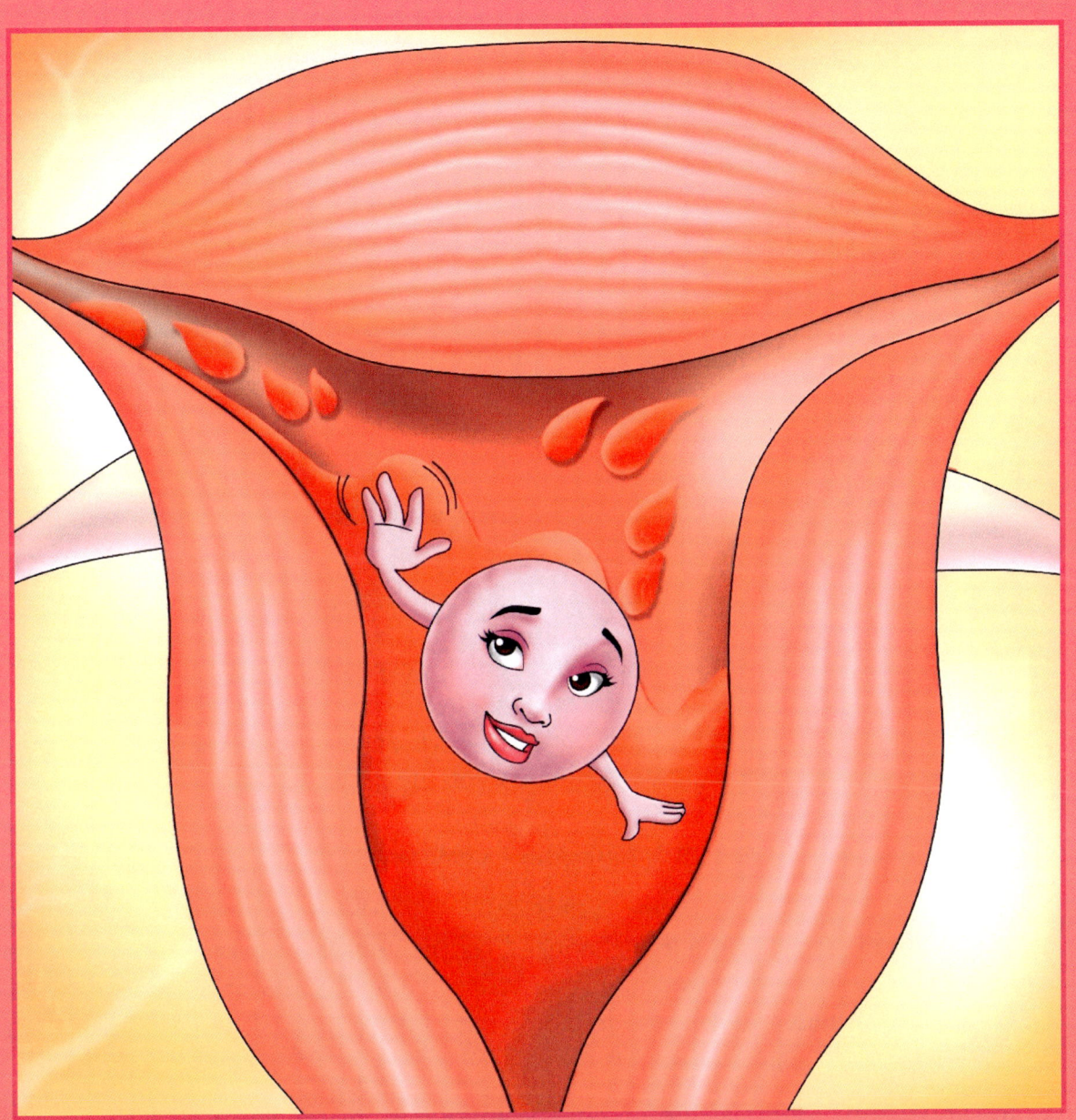

"So I have to go through this every month, huh?" Malia thought aloud. "So far it seems messy, painful, and a nuisance."

"Yeah, it sounds yucky! I don't want a moontime!" Aisha chimed in.

Momma chuckled and put her arm around Malia's shoulder and gave her a squeeze, "Although it may seem that way now, your moontime is wonderful. It comes with many responsibilities because your body is now able to bear children. Giving life to another human being is one of the most beautiful experiences you will ever have… when the time is right. Children are life's highest blessing. Our babies ensure our family will live on forever. Giving birth is something only women can do. It's like having a superpower!"

Aisha looked at her mother with big, brown eyes. "Like the powers of the Kemetic goddess Auset?" she asked.

"Yes, exactly!" Momma responded as she patted the coils of her daughter's ponytails. "You are so smart, Aisha."

"I'd rather have a different superpower like flying or running fast," groaned Malia.

"Every great superpower comes with great responsibilities and sacrifices," Momma said as she hugged her oldest daughter. "The power to create life is the greatest power of all! Women are more sensitive during their moontime, so you might feel grumpy. That's okay, as long as you are respectful to everyone around you. When you feel tired, take some time to be by yourself. Let your body rest. Your moontime is when you are the most creative, so it's a great time to write stories or make artwork.

Your body will go through many changes over the next few years as you continue to grow from a child into an adult. You will develop breasts and hips. You will also grow hair under your arms and in your private area. You will become a powerful young woman."

Malia understood Momma's point, but she still had so many questions!

Mama turned to Aisha. "Malia and I are going to go to the bathroom. I need to show her a few things. Would you like to come, lady bug?"

"Are you going to talk about more moontime stuff?" Aisha was already bored with the subject.

"Yes, we are."

"No ma'am. I'll just wait for Granny. I'm tired of *seeds* and *eggs*!" said Aisha matter-of-factly.

Momma smiled at her as she left the porch with Malia. When they reached the bathroom, Momma pulled out a few boxes from under the sink. Malia was curious.

"I'm sure you've seen these boxes under the sink before, right?" Momma asked.

"Yes, ma'am. I've seen them."

"The boxes I keep under the sink are the products we use to catch our moontime blood. The first choice is a tampon. Tampons are worn inside your *vagina* to soak up the blood. Most are made of cotton. You must be careful if you ever use these. Change them often – at least every four hours. If tampons are left in the *vagina* too long, they may attract germs that can make you very ill with an infection called *T.S.S., Toxic Shock Syndrome*. When you are finished using one, you throw it away.

The second choice is a *menstrual* cup. This also is worn in your *vagina*; it collects blood. When the cup gets full, you can just pour it out and use it again. These are not as dangerous as tampons because they don't attract germs. The third choice, which is the best choice for you at your age, is a maxi pad. The pad is simply stuck inside your panties to catch the blood as it flows out.

It is important that the tampons or pads you use be organic. Most moontime products are sprayed with poisonous chemicals that hurt your body, but the organic ones are much more pure."

Momma's speech was interrupted by the slam of a car door and the familiar sound of Granny prancing up to the house. "Granny!" Malia shrieked with delight as she ran downstairs, leaving her mom to catch up. The girls adored spending time with their grandmother.

Granny was a lively woman with a smile so sunny it could brighten up Malia's crabbiest moods. Malia and Aisha loved her big, tight hugs that always seemed to cloak them with the spicy-sweet scent of cinnamon sticks. The girls thought she was the coolest grandmother ever because she snuck the girls treats when Momma and Daddy weren't looking.

Granny sat down next to Malia and gave her a warm cinnamon hug. "A little birdie told me that you weren't feeling well. My grandbaby is growing up!" she said as she squeezed Malia tightly.

"I'm growing up too!" exclaimed Aisha, refusing to be ignored. She stood up so Granny could see how tall she was.

"Let me see! Yes, I think you have grown a whole foot since last week!" Granny grinned as she winked and pulled Malia even closer. "Your moon cycle brings a lot of changes. You have to know how to take care of yourself: mind, body, and spirit. You must eat well so you and your future babies will be healthy and strong. Although that is a long way off, the habits you create now will affect you for the rest of your life. This is so exciting! Don't worry, I will show you what to do. Come with me."

"Can I go too?" Aisha begged.

"Stay with me for now baby," Momma said. "Granny will be back soon."

Aisha pouted for a moment until Momma kicked the ball in her direction. "Let's play until Granny is finished talking to Malia."

"Okay!" yelled Aisha.

Granny led Malia into the kitchen and started gathering a bunch of food that didn't seem to go well together. Malia was a little worried, but Granny always made great treats. Granny explained, "You must keep your body nourished. The blood that is released during your moontime has a lot of nutrients in it. You must be sure to eat good food so that you can replace them and stay strong and healthy.

One mineral you should be sure to eat often is iron. Iron is important for energy and strength. Many people take organic *food-based vitamins*, but it's also good to get our nutrients from real food."

"What kinds of foods have iron, Granny?" asked Malia. "I hope they don't taste bad."

"Do you like pumpkin seeds, white beans, cacao and dark chocolate, dried apricots, raisins, and leafy green vegetables?"

"Yes. I like chili with beans, I like salad, and I definitely like chocolate!" Malia beamed.

"Cherries are good too. They give you energy, help you rest, and have a little bit of iron in them. Bananas are good to eat during your moontime because they help us feel happy. Pineapples keep your *womb* smelling fresh and sweet. On the other hand, too much processed food, starchy food, sugar, meat, milk, and cheese is not good for your *womb*, so don't eat too much of those things."

"Wow! I really get to eat chocolate?" asked Malia in disbelief.

"As long as you eat the other foods as well," Granny placed her hand on her hip. She looked around slyly before giving Malia a dark chocolate candy. Granny shook her head at Malia playfully, as she placed a handful of spinach, a handful of bright red cherries, two bananas, and a little cacao powder into a blender. She added a bit of coconut water and then pressed the power button. When she was finished, Granny handed Malia a green colored smoothie.

"I have to drink that?" Malia said reluctantly. She tasted a sip. To her surprise, it was yummy! It tasted like chocolate covered cherries. If she closed her eyes, should couldn't even tell the spinach was mixed in there.

When Malia was finished drinking her smoothie, Granny gave her a blanket to take outside. "You shouldn't sit around inside this house all day. You should be out in nature getting sunlight and fresh air," she said. "I will be out in a minute."

Malia took the big, thick blanket and unfolded it under a tall willow tree in her back yard. The freshly cut grass felt cool underfoot. Soon, she spotted Momma walking towards her carrying a tea set and Granny holding a basket. Of course, not far behind was Aisha skipping along merrily. The ladies lounged comfortably on the blanket and Granny poured everyone a cup of tea.

She turned towards Malia "Another way to stay healthy and strong is to use *herbs*. There is a *herb* for almost every condition and there are several that women use specifically for our *wombs*. Red raspberry leaf tones your *womb* and makes it strong. It also helps ease moontime symptoms such as cramping, heavy bleeding, sore breasts, and irregular moon cycles."

"Irregular moon cycles means your moontime takes too long to come or it doesn't come every month. Red raspberry leaf also seems to be able to cheer up grumpy girls as well," Momma snickered as she teased Malia.

Granny smiled, "Exactly. Red raspberry leaf is very easy to take because it has a mild, sweet flavor. You can drink it in a nice tea like this or in a pill. You can even use this tea to make green smoothies. If you take a little bit every day, you will feel much better when your moontime comes.

"I like this tea!" proclaimed Aisha.

"I like it too, sweetheart," Granny agreed. "Ginger is another good tasting *herb* to take for stomach cramps or anytime you feel nauseous. You can drink ginger tea, ginger juice, or add ginger *essential oil* to your lotion and rub it in."

"Ginger is good to season food with too!" added Malia.

"Yes. I love cooking with ginger. It's my secret ingredient," whispered Momma.

"As a matter of fact, I think we're almost out of ginger. I'm going to take Malia to the store to buy some ginger and maxi pads," declared Momma.

"Do you want Aisha and I to get dinner started while you're gone? We should make a special meal for Malia with all of her favorite foods." offered Granny.

"That would be great! I'm sure Aisha would love to have you all to herself," smirked Momma. Granny smiled as Momma turned to walk away. She looked at Aisha and quickly gave her a chocolate candy. Aisha squealed in delight.

"And stop sneaking treats!" Momma exclaimed without turning around. Aisha bent over with laughter. Momma's invisible eyes struck again. Granny was busted!

Momma and Malia walked to the store, enjoying the clear, sunny day. "You need to get used to buying the things you need for your moontime. Some women are embarrassed when they buy pads and things. Remember, your moontime is a sacred time that every woman experiences. There is nothing to be ashamed of," Momma said.

They walked into the store and headed to the feminine hygiene section. Malia was overwhelmed by all the products. As Momma grabbed a box of organic maxi pads, Malia pointed to a box on the shelf.

"What is a dooo-ch?" Malia struggled to pronounce the words on the label.

Momma explained, "Douches (doo-sh-es) are washes that some women use to clean inside their *vaginas*. Most douches have a lot of chemicals in them that are not good for your body. You don't need those. As long as you bathe regularly, wash yourself well, and change your pads frequently, you will smell nice and fresh. A healthy *vagina* keeps itself clean naturally. It's good to let your vagina air out sometimes. That is why we don't wear our panties to bed. Some women use deodorant sprays as well, but those aren't good for you either.

"That sounds simple enough," Malia said as she grabbed a few pieces of ginger and went to check out. She was beginning to feel more confident about caring for herself during her moontime.

When they arrived home, Malia found Granny in the bathroom filling the tub with warm water.

"What are you doing?" asked Malia.

"Teaching you how to smell sweet during your moontime," Granny said with her warm, toothy smile. "Besides rest, food, and *herbs*, hygiene is also very important. You should bathe or shower twice a day - morning and night. Be sure to wash the outside of your *vagina* very well, the inside will clean itself. Your *vagina* is sensitive, so use a natural soap without harsh chemicals."

Granny handed Malia a bar of peppermint soap and continued on, "Blood doesn't have a foul odor. Think about it. When you get a cut it doesn't stink, right? Nonetheless, the bacteria on your body can make moontime blood smell very bad if you are not clean. No one should know your moontime is here because you let yourself get funky," she said as she wrinkled her nose before continuing on.

"Enjoying a warm bath soothes your *womb* during your moontime. We can put *essential oils* in the water, and also in your lotion. Not only do these oils smell great, they also help you to relax and feel better. We can add Epsom salt to your bathwater as well to help soothe aches."

Malia wondered if these oils are what gave Granny her unique cinnamon-spice scent.

Granny pulled out a small, dark bottle and began letting the oil drip slowly into the water. "There are many types of *essential oils* that are great to use during your moontime. This blend has lavender, rose geranium, and clary sage in it. You can create your own blend with your favorite *essential oils*."

The aroma spread across the room. "That smells good!" Malia smiled.

Granny left to help with dinner while Malia got in the tub and started to wash with the fragrant water. She enjoyed all the attention she was getting. The things she was learning from Momma and Granny made her feel like a grown-up. Best of all, she smelled like a bouquet of flowers and her tummy didn't hurt much anymore.

When Malia finished her bath, her home seemed unusually quiet. She was curious what her family was up to. As Malia crept downstairs, she found Granny and Momma sitting on the floor waiting for her. Aisha was sitting in Momma's lap.

"Why are you all meditating?" asked Malia.

Momma patted the rug next to her, "Come join us."

Granny smiled as she explained, "Your moontime is a time to focus on your body, your thoughts, and your emotions. *Meditation* helps you feel calm and cheerful. When we are busy, we don't have time to think as much as we should. It's good to enjoy a few Moments of quiet time."

"Why are you holding rocks?" inquired Malia.

"These are *crystals*. Here, take this one," Momma said as she handed Malia an egg-shaped stone. "This one is called moonstone. *Crystals* have been used for thousands of years to help relieve different conditions. *Crystals*, like all things in nature, have their own energy, and their energy affects us in different ways. Some crystals, like rose quartz and moonstone, are especially good for balancing feminine energy."

"Close your eyes, relax, and listen to your thoughts," said Granny.

Malia began feeling very calm, and soon she felt sleepy. Before she knew it, Malia was fast asleep on the floor, snoring loudly. She was awakened by Momma, Granny, and Aisha's thunderous laughter.

"You snore worse than Daddy!" Aisha snorted.

"Whatever!" Malia responded, trying not to sound embarrassed. She had to admit, she did feel much better than she had earlier. If having her moontime meant drinking delicious smoothies, eating chocolates, having tea parties, smelling good, feeling good, and being surrounded by great women, maybe it wasn't so bad after all. Tending to herself was a lot of responsibility for a young woman, but in return, she had become a very powerful person.

Just then, Malia heard a noise. They all looked towards the front door as it slowly creaked open.

"Daddy! Daddy!" Malia and Aisha exclaimed as he strolled in coolly.

"Good evening ladies," their father said. "My apologies for being late, I stopped to pick up something on the way home."

Momma scurried to greet Daddy. She always seemed to glow when he walked through the door. "Dinner is ready. We waited to eat so we could all celebrate Malia's passage into womanhood," Momma said.

Daddy hugged Momma, and then turned and kissed Granny on the cheek. Aisha climbed on his back while Malia gave him a big hug. "Let go! You are going to squeeze my eyes out!" teased Daddy as his cheeks turned deep shades of crimson. Aisha laughed as she tussled his copper-colored locs.

He handed a box to Malia. She ripped it open and found a stunning cowry shell necklace inside. As Daddy fastened it around her neck he said, "You are precious to me Malia. I have watched you grow from a tiny baby into a lovely young woman. The time has passed by quickly. I am so proud of the person you have become. I wanted to give you this necklace to remind you of that."

Malia felt a little awkward about her father knowing about her moontime, but she cherished the necklace. Daddy's acknowledgment made her feel special.

"No matter how old you get, I will be here for you. Even when you get married and start your own family a long time from now, I will still be here to support and protect you. I love you, baby girl."

"I love you too Daddy!" Malia said as she hugged him even tighter. No matter how old she got, or how many changes she went through, it felt good to know she would always be Daddy's baby girl.

"What about me?" demanded Aisha, still clinging to her father's back.

"I love you too lady bug," Daddy reassured Aisha.

Momma smiled at Malia, "So now that you know all about *menstruation* and how to take care of yourself, how do you feel about your moontime?"

After taking a minute to think, she declared, "My moontime is magnificent!"

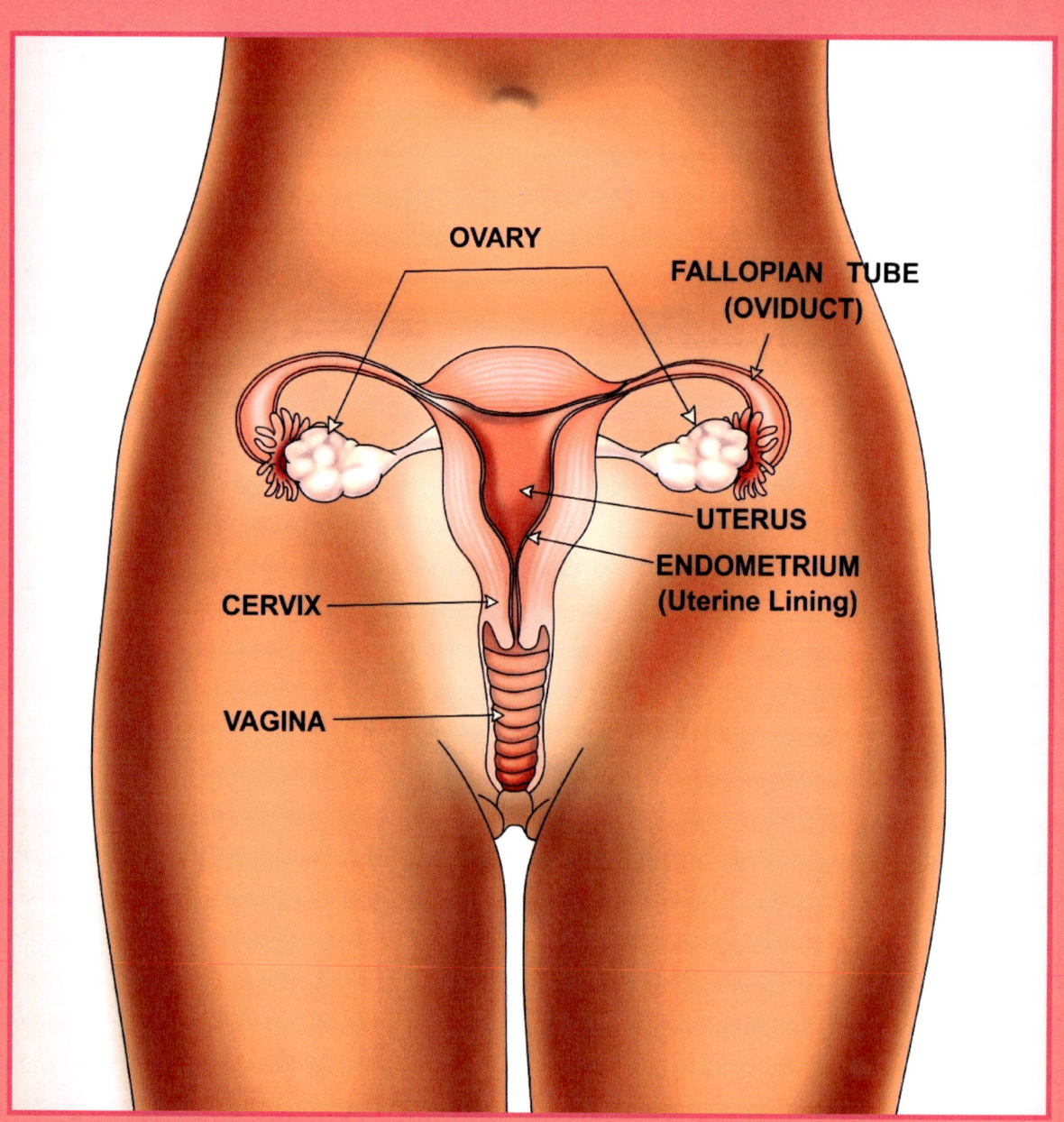

Tampons: These are inserted into the vagina to absorb blood. They are very convenient and allow you to stay active. However, they carry a risk of Toxic Shock Syndrome, especially if they are not changed often. Buy organic tampons to reduce the risk of dangerous chemicals.

Menstrual cups: These are made of a plastic called silicone. These cups are inserted into the vagina to collect blood, which is dumped out later. They are reusable and much safer than tampons, although they may be slightly messier. It may take a little time to learn how to insert them properly.

Maxi Pads: These are stuck onto your underwear to absorb the blood as it leaves your body. These are much safer than tampons and may be more appropriate for girls than tampons or cups. Pads must be changed regularly to reduce the risk of odors and leaks. Buy organic pads to reduce the risk of dangerous chemicals.

Glossary

1. Period- the monthly release of blood from the uterus. This occurs between puberty and menopause in women who are not pregnant.
2. Menstruation- the monthly release of blood from the uterus. This occurs between puberty and menopause in women who are not pregnant.
3. Menstrual- a word to describe something that concerns menstruation.
4. Vagina- the opening that leads from the uterus to the outside of a woman's body.
5. Ovulate/Ovulation- when a woman produces and discharges one or more eggs from an ovary.
6. Womb- a place in which anything is formed or produced, especially the space in a woman's abdomen where babies grow.
7. Egg- the female reproductive cell. When sperm from a man joins with the egg, a baby develops. Also called an ovum.
8. Fallopian tubes- two long, skinny tubes in a woman's abdomen that allow eggs to travel from the ovaries to the uterus. They also provide a tunnel for the sperm to find an egg.
9. Ovary- the place in a woman's body where eggs are made.
10. Seed- another name for a mam's sperm.
11. Sperm- a male reproductive cell. When sperm from a man joins with the egg, a baby develops.
12. Fertilization- when sperm from a man joins with the egg, creating a baby
13. Menopause- the time when a woman's menstruation stops. This often happens between the ages of 45-55 years old.
14. Toxic Shock Syndrome (T.S.S.) - a serious illness that can be caused by wearing tampons too long. The symptoms include fever, upset stomach, rash, and lowered blood pressure. If you think you have T.S.S., go to the hospital right away.
15. Food-based vitamins- these vitamins use foods, such as fruit and vegetables, as the source of nutrition.
16. Herbs- parts of plants that are used to keep us healthy.
17. Essential oils- oils inside plants that helps to keep our minds and bodies healthy.
18. Meditation- a quiet time to be calm and focus on your emotions and your life.
19. Crystals- beautiful stones that are used by people to balance their energy.

Study Guide

Women's Wellness Aids for You to Research:

Feminine Hygiene:

- Menstrual cup
- Menstrual sea sponge
- Organic pads and tampons
- Reusable cloth pads
- Yoni steam

Herbs:

- Alfalfa
- Astragalus
- Chamomile
- Chasteberry
- Cramp bark
- False unicorn
- Ginger
- Lady's mantle
- Maca root
- Motherwort
- Mugwort
- Nettle
- Oatstraw
- Red raspberry leaf
- White peony
- Wild yam

Essential Oils:

- Clary sage
- Evening primrose
- Geranium
- Ginger
- Lavender
- Myrrh
- Rose
- Ylang ylang

Crystals:

- Bloodstone
- Carnelian
- Garnet
- Jade
- Moonstone
- Rose Quartz

Other:

- Castor oil

About the Author

Angela Shabazz is the author of the feminine wellness book for girls, "Malia's Magnificent Moontime". Angela recognized there was a lack of wholesome, health-centered books for children so she decided to create books that taught healthy habits and self-care in a fun way that children could relate to.

Angela has always been fascinated by the human body's natural healing power, and she believes good self-care practices are the ideal way of achieving overall well-being. She loves helping people understand the power of holistic care through her work and writing.

Angela Shabazz is a wife and mother of one child, Kendi. She works as a therapist, life coach, and wellness consultant. She supports women who have experienced prenatal child loss, stillbirth, and/or sexual assault at any age.